D1212967

LUCÍA LACORTE

POOR SPORT

WRITTEN BY
CHRISTIANNE JONES

ILLUSTRATED BY
MARISA MOREA

PICTURE WINDOW BOOKS
a capstone imprint

To Bob and Mike. Thanks for always being such good sports.
–Christianne

Little Boost is published by Picture Window Books
a Capstone Imprint
1710 Roe Crest Drive
North Mankato, Minnesota 56003
www.mycapstone.com

Library of Congress Cataloging-in-Publication Data
Names: Jones, Christianne C., author. | Morea, Marisa, 1982- , illustrator.
Title: Lucia Lacorte, poor sport / by Christianne Jones; [illustrator, Marisa
Morea].
Other titles: Little boost.
Description: North Mankato, Minnesota : Picture Window Books, [2019] |
    Series: Picture window books. Little boost | Summary: Lucia Lacorte's
    gaming club meets on Fridays, but the truth is the other members are not
    having fun because, win or lose, Lucia is a very poor sport; a fact that
    is finally made clear to her when the others stop showing up, and her
    grandfather mimics her behavior when he wins—and loses.
Identifiers: LCCN 2018041110 | ISBN 9781515840282 (hardcover) | ISBN
    9781515840299 (ebook pdf)
Subjects: LCSH: Sportsmanship—Juvenile fiction. | Conduct of life—
    Juvenile fiction. | Human behavior—Juvenile fiction. | CYAC:
    Sportsmanship—Fiction. | Conduct of life—Fiction. | Behavior—Fiction.
Classification: LCC PZ7.J6823 Lu 2019 | DDC 813.6 [E] —dc23
LC record available at https://lccn.loc.gov/2018041110

Designer: Kay Fraser

Printed in the United States of America.
PA49

Lucia Lacorte **LOVED** Fridays.
Why, you ask?

Because the Get Gaming Club met on Fridays,
and Lucia was the founder AND president.

But this Friday, something was <u>STRANGE</u>.
There was a sign outside the GGC's meeting spot.

TRY YOUR BEST
HAVE LOTS OF FUN
🙂 + 🤝
SMILE and SHAKE
when the game is
DONE

You see, Lucia was good at a lot of things.
She REALLY was. Unfortunately, being a good sport
was NOT one of those things.

Obviously, Lucia was a poor sport when she lost.
But she was an even WORSE SPORT when she WON!

A poor sport like Lucia had no time for the sign's rhyme. She RIPPED the sign out of the ground and STOMPED into the room.

"WHO IS RESPONSIBLE FOR THIS?"

TRY YOUR BEST
HAVE LOTS OF FUN
😊 + 🤝
SMILE and SHAKE
when the game is DONE

The room fell silent. The truth was, <u>ALL</u> of the other members had made the sign. Lucia had been spoiling their fun, but they were too scared to tell her.

"If you have a problem with
MY CLUB, then you can just leave,"
Lucia announced. "If not, let's
PLAY SOME GAMES!"

So they played some games,
but NOBODY had fun. Not even Lucia.

The next Friday, Lucia brought a new game to GGC. But nobody was there.

WHERE WERE HER FRIENDS?

"I guess I'll just go home and play this game with Grandpa,"
Lucia said to nobody but herself.

Grandpa was more than happy to
play games with Lucia. However,
things did not go as expected.

Grandpa WON the first game.
He boasted as he DANCED around.

Grandpa WON the second game too.
He chanted as he marched around the room.

"I'M NUMBER ONE! I'M NUMBER ONE!"

"THAT'S <u>NOT</u> VERY NICE, GRANDPA,"
Lucia moaned.

LUCIA won the third game.
But Grandpa was still a poor sport.

"YOU CHEATED! IT'S NOT FAIR!"

"No I didn't! I WON FAIR AND SQUARE," Lucia explained.

"You are not being a GOOD SPORT, Grandpa."

"So what should I do?" he asked.

With that, Lucia had a sudden realization.

"That will be HARD, but I'll give it a TRY," Grandpa replied, trying not to smile. "Now off to bed. Your dad is upstairs waiting for you."

As Lucia got ready for bed, she told her dad
about playing games with Grandpa.

"GRANDPA WAS <u>SO</u> <u>RUDE</u>!" she reported.

"He has a tendency to be a POOR SPORT,"
her dad explained.

"IT WASN'T ANY
FUN, BUT DON'T
WORRY. I TOLD
HIM HOW HE
<u>SHOULD</u> <u>ACT</u>."

"And what exactly did you tell him?" her dad asked.

"I told him to TRY HIS BEST and HAVE LOTS OF FUN. Then SMILE and SHAKE when the game is done," she answered. "IT'S PRETTY SIMPLE."

The next day, Lucia called an emergency GGC meeting.

"I HAVE AN ANNOUNCEMENT. I'VE BEEN A POOR SPORT, AND I'M SORRY."

Once again, the room fell silent.

But then a SLOW CLAP started, followed by CHEERS.

Her friends forgave her and couldn't wait to play games again.

"AND FROM NOW ON, WE WILL START
EVERY MEETING WITH OUR NEW PLEDGE,"
Lucia announced.

"LET THE GAMES BEGIN!"